Pet Charms

Here, Kitty, Kitty

by Amy Edgar

illustrated by Jomike Tejido

SCHOLASTIC INC.

Library of Congress Cataloging-in-Publication Data

Names: Edgar, Amy, author. | Tejido, Jomike, illustrator.
Title: Here, kitty, kitty / by Amy Edgar ; illustrated by Jomike Tejido.
Description: New York, NY : Scholastic Inc., 2017. | Series: Pet charms ; #3
Summary: Molly's cat Stella is behaving oddly, but Molly cannot find her special magic bracelet that
allows her to understand what animals are saying, so she does not know what Stella is trying to tell her.
Identifiers: LCCN 2016040568 | ISBN 9781338045918 (pbk.)
Subjects: LCSH: Cats—Behavior—Juvenile fiction. | Magic—Juvenile fiction.
Bracelets—Juvenile fiction. | Human-animal communication—Juvenile fiction. | CYAC: Cats—Fiction.
Magic—Fiction. | Bracelets—Fiction. | Human-animal communication—Fiction.
Classification: LCC PZ7.E225 He 2017
DDC [E]--dc23 LC record available at https://lccn.loc.gov/2016040568

ISBN 978-1-1338-04591-8

10 9 8 7 6 5 4 3 2 1   17 18 19 20 21

Printed in China
First edition, July 2017
Book design by Steve Ponzo

Molly had a magic bracelet.

She did not wear it all the time.

But when she did, she could understand animals.

No one knew her secret.

Molly and her best friend, Lexie, were playing a game.
Then Molly's cat, Stella, walked by.
She meowed.

"What's up with Stella today?" asked Lexie.
"She usually comes over to say hi."

"Hmmm," said Molly. "She _is_ acting a little strange."

"I wish Stella could tell us what's wrong," said Molly.

"That would be cool!" said Lexie.

Then Molly remembered her magic bracelet.

She looked in the drawer where she kept it.

"Oh no!" said Molly. "My bracelet is missing."

"Don't worry," said Lexie. "We'll find it."

"I know I wore it yesterday," said Molly.

The girls looked all over Molly's room.

But they did not find the bracelet.

Lexie leaned down to pet Stella.
But the cat ran away.
"That's strange," said Lexie.
"Stella loves to be petted."

The girls searched the kitchen next.
But they did not find the bracelet.
Stella hid under the table.

Molly saw Stella's food dish.

"Look, Lexie," she said. "Stella did not eat her food.

"Maybe she's not feeling well," said Lexie.

Stella meowed loudly.

Molly wished she had her magic bracelet.

Then she could understand Stella's meow

"Hey, we were at Paws Palace yesterday," said Lexie.
"I bet your bracelet is there!"
Molly remembered talking to the hamster.
"Let's go!" said Molly. "Plus, we can ask Aunt Vera
about Stella. She knows everything about animals."

Molly leaned down.

"Stella, here is your favorite blanket," she said.

Stella meowed louder than ever.

Then she hid farther under the table.

The friends ran to Paws Palace.

Molly waved at Mr. Wiggles.

She had saved the puppy during a rainstorm.

He had given her the magic bracelet.

Molly rang the bell.

"Hello, girls," said Aunt Vera. "Come on in."

"Hi, Aunt Vera!" they said.

"Have you seen my charm bracelet?" asked Molly.
"No," said Aunt Vera. "But you were here yesterda
You fed the turtles and gave Mr. Wiggles a bath."

"That's it!" shouted Molly.

She raced to the bathroom.

The bracelet was right next to the tub.

Molly put on the sparkly bracelet.
Now she could understand animals.
"Running in circles makes me thirsty,"
squeaked the hamster.
Molly refilled his water bottle.
"You are even faster today," Molly whispered.
She loved helping animals.

"Aunt Vera, we're worried about Stella," said Molly.

"I hope I can help," said Aunt Vera. "What's wrong?"

"She doesn't want to hang out," said Lexie.

"She won't let us pet her," added Molly.

"And she didn't eat her food today," said Lexie.

"That doesn't sound like Stella," said Aunt Vera.
"Maybe I should come take a look?"
Molly agreed.
She was worried about her pet.

Molly, Lexie, and Aunt Vera walked to Molly's house.
They went to the kitchen, but Stella wasn't there.
"Here, kitty, kitty," they called over and over.
They looked everywhere for Stella.

They sat down to think.

"Where could she be?" asked Aunt Vera.

That's when they heard soft meowing.

"It's coming from your closet," said Lexie.

Molly opened the door . . .

. . . and she found Stella curled up with three kittens

"Stella, you're a mom?!" said Molly.

"Now we know why she was acting strangely,"
said Lexie.

"Yes, she was about to have kittens!" said Aunt Vera

24

Molly scratched Stella behind the ears.

"You did a great job," Molly whispered. "I am so sorry I couldn't understand you earlier."

"The blanket you left was purrrrfect," purred Stella.

"Girls, do you see how the mama cat made a nest?" asked Aunt Vera. "It's important for newborn kittens to stay warm and cozy."

"Look, Molly!" said Lexie. "Your blanket is part of Stella's nest."

The girls giggled.

Molly brought Stella food and water.
Then they all watched Stella lick her kittens.
The tiny kittens fell back to sleep.

Molly went back over to the closet.
"I will take good care of your kittens,"
she told Stella.
"I know you will," said Stella.

Just then, Molly saw her bracelet sparkle brightly.
She blinked.
A new kitten charm was hanging from it!

"I can't wait to hold the kittens," said Lexie.
"Me too!" said Molly. "Aunt Vera, when can we
pick them up?"
"In a week," said Aunt Vera. "They should stay
with their mom for now."

Wow, this was an exciting day," said Lexie.

Yes, it was," agreed Molly.

We found your bracelet — and kittens!" said Lexie.

I love having three new animal friends!" said Molly.

31